OLD WOLF

The Barn

Blue Heron

The Christmas Rat

*Hard Gold: The Colorado
Gold Rush of 1859*

*Iron Thunder: The Battle Between
the* Monitor *& the* Merimac

Night Journeys

A Place Called Ugly

The Secret School

Something Upstairs

*Sometimes I Think
I Hear My Name*

Old Wolf

A FABLE

By
AVI

Illustrated by
BRIAN FLOCA

A Richard Jackson Book
Atheneum Books for Young Readers
NEW YORK LONDON TORONTO SYDNEY NEW DELHI

ATHENEUM BOOKS FOR YOUNG READERS | An imprint of Simon & Schuster Children's Publishing Division | 1230 Avenue of the Americas, New York, New York 10020 | This book is a work of fiction. Any references to historical events, real people, or real places are used fictitiously. Other names, characters, places, and events are products of the author's imagination, and any resemblance to actual events or places or persons, living or dead, is entirely coincidental. | Text copyright © 2015 by Avi | Illustrations copyright © 2015 by Brian Floca | Text material from *Archery: Steps to Success, Third Edition* by Kathleen M. Haywood and Catherine F. Lewis, and *Archery Fundamentals* by Douglas Engh, reprinted with permission from Human Kinetics, Inc. | All rights reserved, including the right of reproduction in whole or in part in any form. | ATHENEUM BOOKS FOR YOUNG READERS is a registered trademark of Simon & Schuster, Inc. | Atheneum logo is a trademark of Simon & Schuster, Inc. | For information about special discounts for bulk purchases, please contact Simon & Schuster Special Sales at 1-866-506-1949 or business@simonandschuster.com. | The Simon & Schuster Speakers Bureau can bring authors to your live event. For more information or to book an event, contact the Simon & Schuster Speakers Bureau at 1-866-248-3049 or visit our website at www.simonspeakers.com. | The illustrations for this book are rendered in pencil. | The text for this book is set in Chaparral Pro. | Manufactured in the United States of America | 0715 FFG | First Edition | 10 9 8 7 6 5 4 3 2 1 | Library of Congress Cataloging-in-Publication Data | Avi, 1937– | Old wolf / Avi ; illustrated by Brian Floca. — First edition. | pages cm | "A Richard Jackson book." | Summary: "A wolf and bird must fight the starving time and find food, while a human boy learns to hunt."—Provided by publisher. | ISBN 978-1-4424-9921-8 (hardcover) | ISBN 978-1-4424-9924-9 (eBook) | 1. Wolves—Juvenile fiction. [1. Wolves—Fiction. 2. Ravens—Fiction. 3. Friendship—Fiction. 4. Hunting—Fiction.] I. Floca, Brian, illustrator. II. Title. | PZ10.3.A965Ol 2015 | [Fic]—dc23 | 2014003381

FOR RICHARD JACKSON

—*Avi & Brian*

— N —→

Bend Valley

County Road #61

← Clarksville P.O. and store
6 miles

← School
6 miles

← Lockport 17 miles

← Philbeck 21 miles

6 miles

Moose Mountain Range
Wolf pack
den x
Iron
Mountain
Casey's
x home
Bend Valley
Pass
Lodgepole
National Forest
Rock Ridge x
Trail Head
Altitude
8 miles

OLD WOLF

1

I T WAS THE STARVING TIME.

Not the end of winter. Not the start of spring. Not cold. Not hot. Daylight and nightdark were almost equal. Mud lay here and snow lay there. It was as if Earth herself could not decide between life and death.

2

In the high country, on a late afternoon in the month of March, the eight gray wolves of the Iron Mountain pack—Tonagan, Garby, Nikito, Pildown, Debalt, the two pups—Conall and Onai—and the pack leader, the old wolf called Nashoba—lay before their den, a cold, shallow hollow in an outcropping of dull red rock.

Nashoba was allowing his two five-week-old blue-eyed pups to tumble about him, yapping and squealing. Nonetheless, he was worried. The wolves in the pack had not eaten for two weeks—not so much as a chipmunk or a vole. They were hungry and increasingly tense.

The pups most concerned Nashoba. Originally, the litter had been three in number. One had died. Needing something more than Tonagan's milk to survive, Conall and Onai were already mouthing

Nashoba's muzzle, their way of begging for meat. Where, he fretted, was he going to get it?

While Nashoba lay deep in thought, Garby— three years old, and the largest, strongest wolf in the pack—suddenly called out, "Nashoba! It's time *I* was pack leader."

Taken by surprise, but choosing to act as if he had not heard the challenge, Nashoba did not move.

The other wolves did. The adults got up swiftly and backed away. Even the pups, sensing something amiss, scrambled to their mother, who nosed them behind her for safety.

"You are our pack leader, Nashoba," snarled Garby. "But you just sit here playing with your pups. You should be leading us in a hunt."

Uncertain what the outcome might be if he fought the much younger wolf, Nashoba remained absolutely still.

Garby, taking the old wolf's response to be weakness, leaped to his feet. "We're hungry, Nashoba!" he barked. "We need food. If you can't lead us to it, I will!"

Nashoba spread his toes a little and gazed

steadily at Garby with his deep golden eyes. "Are you challenging *me*?" he asked, in a soft, rumbly voice. He knew the answer to the question perfectly well but was hoping Garby would back down.

All Garby did was snarl, "We know the truth, Nashoba. You're too old to lead."

The words stung Nashoba. *How dare the young wolf speak so!*

With a deep-chested growl, the old wolf came slowly to his feet and stood with legs stiff, neck hairs raised, and tail high. He wanted to give Garby time to retreat.

Garby, however, held his place and continued to stare directly into the pack leader's eyes, which, among wolves, is a blatant challenge. "Admit it, Nashoba," he said. "You've become useless!"

Nashoba drew back his lips to show his teeth, and took a step toward the strong young wolf.

The other wolves moved farther away.

"You don't frighten me, Nashoba!" Garby spat out.

Knowing he must act quickly or lose all respect, Nashoba lunged at the young wolf's neck.

With the deftness of youth, Garby slipped to

one side, causing Nashoba to miss. At the same moment, he dove, gripped Nashoba's right front paw in his mouth, and bit down, hard.

Nashoba, ignoring the piercing pain, twisted about, reached up, and grasped Garby's neck in his jaws. He began to squeeze, tighter and tighter.

With a gasp, Garby released Nashoba's paw and dropped to the ground.

Panting, Nashoba let go of the young wolf but stood over him, undecided what to do. Choosing to be generous, as befit a pack leader, he lifted his bloody paw and placed it on the back of Garby's neck.

The young wolf whined in pleading submission.

That was enough for Nashoba. Pleased with himself, he stepped away but glanced pointedly at the other wolves. One by one, they lowered their heads and tails in wordless acknowledgment of the old wolf's leadership.

Nashoba, not wishing to reveal how much pain his paw was giving him, how shaken he was, how rapidly his heart was pounding, turned his back on the pack and walked into the woods—slowly.

When he was some forty yards from the den—

beyond the pack's view—the old wolf flopped to the ground, stretched his feet before him, and allowed himself a deep, deep breath.

3

When Nashoba regained his composure, he examined his paw closely. Garby's bite had been not just painful but deep, far worse than the old wolf had realized. First, he licked the oozing blood, cleaning and soothing the hurt. Then he rested his chin on the earth between his front legs. Eyes closed, he sought to ignore the ache—the ache in his paw and the ache in his heart. *How dare young Garby challenge me!*

In the wild, wolves can live for as long as nine years, sometimes more. Nashoba was eight. He weighed some eighty pounds (down from a hundred and ten) and was thirty-five inches tall at his shoulder and just less than four feet long, not including his tail.

The gray fur on his back—it had become much grayer as of late—and along the top of his tapered nose was soft and thick, except for the stiff, gray muzzle hairs. His chest and belly fur was white but tinged delicately with brown; his ears were dark and rounded, and his golden eyes, encircled by black markings, had ebony pupils.

Nashoba was well aware that he had come close to being overthrown as pack leader. The next time Garby challenged him—as he surely would— the young wolf might be successful. *But the life of the Iron Mountain pack depends on me,* Nashoba told himself. *I am not too old to hunt. Or kill.*

But Nashoba knew that now he must prove it— and soon.

4

Next morning, when the first glow of dawn touched the summit of Iron Mountain, Nashoba stood on a high ridge looking down into the still shadowy Bend Valley.

Over the past two weeks, the old wolf had hunted for food in many places, but without success. The animals the wolves fed on—deer, elk, and moose—were more than likely in the lower valley, where they had gone to wait out winter. That area, however, was where humans lived.

Though wolves never attacked humans, Nashoba was well aware that humans attacked wolves. Not only were these humans crafty, they were able to kill from great distances. All wolves knew to fear them.

Moreover, the last time Nashoba had ventured into the lower valley—two weeks ago—he had come upon an old human with white hair. At first Nashoba had thought that the human had been heading toward the pack's den. He had been just about to race home to give warning when the human had veered away.

No, the deep valley was too dangerous for Nashoba. He needed to find another place to hunt.

But where?

He looked up. Branches of lodgepole pine, spruce, and still-leafless aspen crisscrossed over his head like a spider's web. Higher still, the sky was as gray as his fur. To either side of Bend Valley, mountain peaks glistened with melting snow. To the west, the last of the three-quarter moon—pale white and growing fainter—was sinking into the horizon.

Nashoba looked left and right. He listened. He sniffed. Yet he did *not* hear, smell, or see anything to tell him where any large animals might be.

Undecided, the old wolf was standing perfectly still on a quilt of dirty snow and mud, an area spotted with pools of cold water that lay as mute as dark mirrors, when he heard: *"Caw! Caw! Caw!"*

It was the call of a raven.

Nashoba tilted his ears forward and listened intently.

The call repeated itself. *"Caw! Caw! Caw!"*

As the wolf was aware, ravens had a well-deserved reputation for two things: playing tricks, and warning of death. Some wolves believed the birds were enchanted. Whatever the truth, Nashoba was also aware that ravens often knew the location of moose, elk, and deer. For their own reasons, ravens were interested in what wolves hunted.

Perhaps, thought Nashoba, *this raven is sending a message.*

Unfortunately, the bird's call came from deep in the valley, precisely where the wolf did not want to go. Besides, the thought of depending on anyone—another wolf or some *bird*—was not to his liking.

Nashoba was not sure what to do. As pack leader, he was obliged to defend the pack, to keep all in health, to avoid danger, and to maintain good order. Those duties fulfilled, his dignity as leader would be respected, and every wolf in the pack would know his or her place. But this would not happen unless his pack was fed.

Nashoba looked about again. The sky promised change. He sensed dampness and a northern wind. Though late for snow, spring storms were always a possibility in the high country. That prospect added even more urgency to his need. Snow—or rain—would make his hunting that much more difficult.

The old wolf lifted his right front paw and

studied it. The wound was now covered by dried blood. It still gave pain, but not, he decided, so much. He was sure he could still run, still hunt.

Garby's taunt *You are useless!* seeped into his thoughts. Simultaneously, the raven's call—*"Caw! Caw!"*—rang out again like the tolling of a bell. Its message—its *possible* message—that food was to be found was too tempting.

Very well: Nashoba would find the raven and see why it had called.

Decision made, the old wolf began to trot down into the valley.

5

That same morning, Casey Seton opened his eyes to his thirteenth birthday. Warm and snug beneath his thick down quilt, he enjoyed the moment. *I'm so much older!* he told himself. *No longer just a kid! A teenager! An adult . . . almost.*

Images of the next few months spooled out in his mind like a movie trailer: a sweet spring and glorious summer, liberty to wander through the forest, fishing, hunting, and swimming. Doing whatever he liked. Then he would start high school in Lockport, where he would have a new life with new friends.

"It'll be your last free summer," his dad had told him.

Startled, Casey had said, "What happens after that?"

His father had laughed. "An old guy like you might want to find a summer job. Earn your keep."

Casey had taken that as a joke.

Rolling over, he gazed at the posters on his wall: a great bull elk with twelve-point antlers; a keen-eyed Ute warrior, his bow drawn; a fully bearded old-time trapper, hair braided, dressed in a buck-skin jacket, a muzzle-loading musket cradled in his arms.

Casey's greatest desire—beyond all else—was to be a hunter.

He glanced at his bedside clock. Seven a.m.

Schooltime. The boy sighed. His old life was still with him. In fact, the next moment, his mother poked her head into his room.

Bess Seton was a small woman with a curly mop of strawberry-blond hair, blue eyes, and a quick smile.

"Morning, love!" she called. "Do teenagers go to school?" Her laughter tumbled forth the way Casey loved it, full of mischief and challenge. "Presents are waiting!" she added before retreating.

"I'm coming!" Casey shouted, and jumped out of bed.

First, as always, he reeled up the window blind and checked the weather. The view was mostly of Lodgepole National Forest, crowned by Iron Mountain. That lonely peak—eight miles beyond Casey's home and more than eleven thousand feet high with bare rock at the summit—was capped with snow.

"The biggest backyard in the world," Casey's dad had called the forest. He and Casey had often hunted and fished there. The whole family hiked, camped, and had climbed Iron Mountain multiple

times. Casey knew the land as well as his home, at least the first few miles of it.

Their modern log house stood at Bend Valley Pass, on a quarter-mile dirt road off County Highway Sixty-One. The Setons' nearest neighbors were down-valley, half a mile away. Sixty-One went on for only another quarter-mile, and then ended at the Rock Ridge Trailhead. The trailhead led hikers and hunters into the national forest and real high country.

Casey studied the gray sky. *Weather coming,* he thought.

"Getting late, Case!" he heard his mother call.

A barefooted race to the bathroom: teeth brushing, a pass of cold water over his rosy face, a comb swipe through reddish hair, the slinging on of clothes—he hated scratchy new clothing—and Casey was done.

He ran to the kitchen and the smell of bacon and coffee. Troy Seton, Casey's dad—big shouldered, broad faced, and brown bearded—was already in his Carhartt work clothes, cap on his head. He leaned back against the fridge, a mug of coffee in one large hand, a muffin in the other.

Casey's dad worked 24/7 for the Valley Power Company, repairing whatever was broken in Rickles County, an area of some 2,300 square miles. Repairs might be in a townhouse or a downed line in the middle of the wilderness. Wilderness took up half the county.

Casey's mom was postmaster in Clarksville, a small town twelve miles down-valley where his school was located. Now she was at the stove making a cheddar cheese omelet with Marco's Red Hot Sauce—Casey's favorite.

"Happy birthday, Casey!" his parents cried in ragged unison when he walked in.

Casey grinned. A plate on the breakfast counter was set with two blueberry muffins and bacon alongside glasses of orange juice and milk. A gift-wrapped something sat next to it.

For a moment Casey's spirits sagged. The gift looked like a book. *A book!* He truly liked to read, but he had been hoping—expecting—something else.

His father gestured toward the present. "That's just for starters. Come on. Don't want to be late for school."

Casey snatched up the package and tore away the red-white-and-blue-striped wrapping paper. He found two books: *Archery: Steps to Success* and *Archery Fundamentals*.

The instant he read the titles, his mood soared and his head filled with one thought: *All right! I'm going to be a hunter!*

His dad, eyes full of merriment, said, "They should help you with your video game."

6

Following a narrow animal trail that led into the valley, Nashoba trotted steadily on his long thin legs. With each step, his five-inch-wide paw pads marked the soft earth as if to brand the land as his own.

Though he kept alert for the raven, he saw no sign. *How far should he go?* He kept reminding himself that if the raven *did* know something, that knowledge would solve his pack's food problem. And his own.

The raven's cry came again: *"Caw! Caw!"*

The bird was still lower in the valley.

Nashoba went on.

7

Casey finished his breakfast and ran back to his room, clutching his new books tightly. He knew he had to hurry, but he could not resist sitting at his desk and clicking on his computer. His favorite video game, Bowhunter, popped up, the screen filling with a jungle scene: green vines, immense multicolored flowers, tall green grasses, and dangling black snakes. There were animals, too—lions, wolves, and tigers to shoot at, as well as hawks, ravens, and buzzards. At the bottom of the screen, an arrow tip pointed toward the jungle, and at the animals and birds when they suddenly appeared as targets.

Left hand: the button *W* to move forward, *A* to move left, *D* right, *S* back. Right hand: the mouse to point the arrow now in one direction, then another. Ready to run, jump, crouch, if necessary.

When he clicked the *W* button, the jungle began to move toward him, creating the illusion that he was walking forward. Casey watched for creatures, ready to shoot the moment he spotted one.

A zebra bounced by.

Casey aimed, clicked his mouse, and the arrow shot forward, trailing a bloodred line. The zebra fell, feet straight up, looking like an upside-down table.

Great shot! said an automated voice, while the words KILL SCORE: 1 came up on the screen.

Casey kept watching.

A large raven appeared hunched on the branch of tree.

Just as Casey aimed and was about to click the mouse, the bird spread its wings and flew away.

You must be quicker, said the computer voice. *Kill score—one.*

Casey waited. As always, the bird reappeared, this time in the upper-right corner of his screen. Casey shifted the arrow, aimed, and clicked the mouse. The arrow leaped across the screen. The bird tumbled.

Great shot! said the automated voice, and the words KILL SCORE: 2 came up.

I'm good at this! thought Casey. *I can kill anything.*

8

A tiny rustling sound off the trail brought Nashoba to a halt. He cocked his ears and sniffed, his black nose all but vibrating. A mouse! The thought of food made his mouth water. Though his sore leg trembled, he held motionless, front paws together, eyes intent on the ground. Then he reared and pounced.

His paws came down on . . . nothing.

All he had gained was misery in his foot. With

a whine of frustration and a shake of his head, Nashoba continued along the trail.

How far, he wondered, *should I go?*

Remembering how the pups mouthed him, begging for meat, Nashoba knew the answer: *until I find food.*

9

"We're going to be late!" Casey's mother called.

Casey grabbed his backpack and one of the archery books, then hurried out of his room. He wished he did not have school and instead could stay home with his jungle game and hunt. The next moment he reminded himself: *Tomorrow I'll be able to play all morning.*

10

Nashoba was deep in the valley. Daylight had brightened. Small white clouds eased through the trees only to fade away like shy ghosts. Blue shadows slid across the land even as they shrank in size. Birds chirped randomly. Snowmelt flowed.

Now and again the old wolf lifted his nose. The wind had shifted. It was coming from the north now, behind him. The shift not only limited his depth of smell, it all but assured a big change in the weather. Another frustration.

Nashoba halted to sniff a bush, then a boulder. There were elk scent markings but nothing recent. He listened. *Where was that raven?* He waited.

"*Caw! Caw!*"

The bird was closer but still farther down valley. Nashoba hesitated. The lower he went, the more likely he would come upon humans.

I can avoid them, he told himself, and kept on.

11

Backpack stuffed with schoolbooks in one hand, archery book in the other, Casey climbed into the shotgun seat of his mom's old SUV. At the same time, his dad got into his Ford panel truck, parked alongside.

Casey's mom rolled down her window and called to her husband, "Where you working today, honey?"

"A line is sparking over by Philbeck."

"See if you can get home early. Weather is coming, and I think we've got a birthday dinner tonight."

Troy looked past Bess to his son, and grinned. "Wouldn't miss it for anything."

"Be safe!" she called to him—what she said every time he went off.

Troy's diesel motor truck rumbled to life, idled for a short time, and then began to bump and bounce down the dirt road.

Casey's mom followed. The moment her SUV moved onto the tar-smooth county road south to Clarksville, Casey flipped open his new book. His eyes took in the first words:

You must learn how to handle archery equipment safely. Target archers and bowhunters alike must be aware of the harm an arrow can do if they do not exercise care at all times.

The text went on.

When we were kids, the local police department gave a demonstration on the park archery range. A policeman filled a gallon jug with sand and placed a balloon behind it. He fired a handgun into the jug. The sand stopped the bullet. An archer shot an arrow into the jug. It passed through the sand and popped the balloon. The policeman made his point to would-be archers: an arrow can be lethal when shot from a bow.

Casey stopped reading and stared out the window, thrilled at the thought of all that power.

12

Nashoba jogged along the forest trail for two more miles but saw nothing of the raven. He had traveled six miles now and was tired. His paw was throbbing. When he drew near a clearing that he recognized, he stopped, unsure about continuing.

He sniffed the air but if there were animals—or humans—in or beyond the clearing, the back-blowing breeze did not bring him any clue. He remained motionless, watching and listening intensely, only to have the silence broken by a brash *Caw!*

The raven was close.

Nashoba waited. Once again the raven's cry came: *"Caw, Caw!"*

Is it a warning or a welcome? Nashoba wondered. He moved to the edge of the clearing then halted to study the open space. It was almost ninety yards end to end. Opposite where he stood, the ground rose into a hill covered with leafless aspen trees. The center earth looked muddy from runoff from the hill. Here and there, stinkweed had begun to poke up, looking like green flames.

To the left was a small pond, walled in on the far side by a border of high grass, still brown. Two thin disks of ice floated on the still waters. The pond surface mirrored the trees on the hill so perfectly, it was hard to know what was real, what was a reflection. As Nashoba looked on, a pair of red-winged blackbirds called to each other from the tall grass.

Sensing nothing to fear, Nashoba stepped into the clearing.

Next to the pond stood an ancient aspen, its lower trunk encircled by crusty gray bark. One branch reached over the pond. As Nashoba looked, a raven flew onto it. A female, he was sure of it.

She was a big bird—some twenty-four inches in length. Completely black, her feathers glistened with an ebony sheen. The large, pointy, and slightly curved bill—its base partly covered with feathers— was just as black. Around her neck, feathers were

shaggy. Each of her black legs had four sharp talons, which gripped the branch tightly. The tail was wedge shaped. *Her eyes are black and beady—bright*, Nashoba thought, *with the knowledge of something*.

He studied the bird suspiciously.

The raven leaned toward him. *"Caw!"* she cried. "You took your time, wolf! I've been waiting quite a while."

To Nashoba's ears, the bird's voice was loud, coarse, and rude.

Not wanting her to think he had come merely because *she* called, Nashoba ambled to the edge of the pond and casually lapped some cold water. It eased his hunger.

His drink done, he kept his head low, the better to scan the pond. Perhaps there would be a fish or a frog to eat.

"It's still too cold for frogs!" the raven squawked.

Irritated that the bird had guessed what he was thinking, Nashoba made no reply.

Nonetheless, the bird leaned forward, opened her beak, extended her black tongue, and made clacking noises. "In case you didn't know," she said, "it'll take two more weeks of good weather before the frogs start peeping." She cocked her head to one side. "Would you, Nashoba, leader of the Iron Mountain pack, really eat a frog?"

Ignoring the gibe but pleased that the bird knew who and what he was, the wolf glanced up. "Do I know you?"

The raven sidestepped toward the end of the branch, her weight causing it to bow down closer to Nashoba's head.

"My name is Merla," said the raven.

"And you have heard of me," said Nashoba.

"I know everything about this forest."

"*Everything?*"

Merla bobbed her head. "We ravens are smart. The smartest."

Nashoba, annoyed by the raven's conceit, did not reply.

"Everybody knows how smart we are," said the bird. "No creatures in the world are as clever as ravens."

"What about wolves?"

"*Caw!*" cried Merla, and to Nashoba it sounded

like laughter. "I know many things," the raven went on, cocking her head to the side. "And one of them is that it's not smart to argue with someone who wants to help you."

"You're just a bird," snapped Nashoba. "How can a bird help a wolf like me?" He sat, tail extended, and deliberately kept his eyes on the pond. The pair of red-winged blackbirds fluttered about, their red shoulder marks flashing like flaring flames. The wolf wondered if the birds had built a nest, and if there were eggs in it. He would be glad to eat one— or two.

The raven remained quiet for a few moments and studied Nashoba. Then she said, "When a wolf sits by a cold pond willing to eat slimy frogs and small bird eggs, I'd say he's *very* hungry."

How did she guess my thoughts again? Nashoba wondered. All he said, however, was, "Better to eat than to starve."

"What an original idea!" the bird cried mockingly. "But I imagine you'd be interested if I told you there was a small herd of elk not far from here. No bulls, Nashoba, just cows and calves—the calves so young, they are still spotted. "*Caw!*" cried the raven. "*Very* tender and tasty, to be sure."

Nashoba, trying to contain his eagerness, waited before saying, "I suppose I might be interested."

"*I suppose you might,*" echoed Merla, her voice thick with sarcasm. "I suppose you just *might*," she said again, and made two quick scratchy rubs of her bill on the branch as if to sharpen her wit. "And you and I *might* be of use to each other."

"Not likely," Nashoba said.

"Don't be a worm-wit, wolf!" cried the raven. "You know perfectly well what I'm suggesting. When wolves kill, ravens feast."

Now, Nashoba knew that when wolves were successful in a hunt, ravens quickly gathered at the remains. They liked to eat what wolves killed. He found the practice contemptible. That he might be beholden to such a creature was offensive to him.

"Wolf!" cried the raven. "Think! It's almost spring. The elk don't have much energy. The bull is nowhere in sight or smell of his harem. Just cows, Nashoba, just cows and their calves." She leaned forward. "And the calves are defenseless.

Sometimes they are even left alone. Easy food, old wolf. Yours for the taking!"

The word *food* made Nashoba's stomach rumble. *But to take advice from a bird . . .* Then he thought to himself, *The pack needn't know how I found elk.* He looked up. "Show me," he said as casually as he could.

Merla, head to one side, gazed at the wolf with her beady black eyes. She was enjoying the moment. Then she gave a loud *Caw!* and leaped into the air.

Once airborne, she made a sharp turn, extending her wings their full four feet until her feathery tips stuck out like individual fingers. *Whoosh-whoosh.* Looking like her own shadow, she flew in a southerly direction.

Nashoba had to scramble to keep her in sight.

13

Everybody in the small Clarksville school knew it was Casey's thirteenth birthday. Mrs. Washington, the principal, announced it on the PA system first thing that morning, as she did for all kids' birthdays. Then his classroom teacher, Ms. Oates, had the class sing the usual song. They even did the "Stand up and show us your pretty face!" part. Though Casey thought it babyish, he went along, grinning. Even so, what he wanted to say was, *I'm not a kid anymore. I'm a teenage hunter.*

Casey's favorite class was geometry. For him the charts and graphs were really mapmaking, and he loved it. As he worked out problems and measured lines, he imagined he was finding his way through the forest, on the trail, deeper into the game.

14

Nashoba followed Merla for two more miles but halted when he lost sight of her. He was breathing hard, mouth open, tongue extended, legs unsteady with effort. His front right paw throbbed and his tail drooped. While rushing through the woods, clumps of his winter underfur had caught on bushes. He began to think, *This raven is mocking me.*

Noticing a patch of crusty old snow, he went to it, swallowed a mouthful, and lay down. The cold wetness soothed his chest. He rubbed his face in it. Then he looked around.

The valley trees—fewer pine, more aspen, and some cottonwoods—were clustered together. A multitude of tiny leaf buds infused the air with a hazy green.

Detecting no hint of elk, Nashoba told himself that ravens were not to be trusted. *You can only depend on yourself.*

Even as he had the thought, he felt a sharp pain on the tip of his tail. He leaped and whirled about only to see a flutter of black wings.

Merla had pecked him. The bird, now on a bush, leaned toward him and stuck out her black tongue.

"Caw! Caw!" She laughed. "I thought wolves were faster than that. Just how old are you? *Nine?*"

"Never mind my age," snapped Nashoba, struggling to keep his temper. "Where are those elk?"

"Oh my! Your sense of smell has grown weak too. Really, how old *are* you?"

"Where are the elk?" Nashoba demanded.

"I'd say you were at *least* nine," said Merla.

"Where?" snarled Nashoba.

Merla ruffled her neck feathers, leaned again toward the wolf, and said, "What about your eyesight? That failing too?"

"Do you or do you not know about elk?" cried Nashoba.

"Of course I do."

Glowering, Nashoba pulled back his black lips and exposed his sharp teeth, almost all forty-two of them.

Instead of retreating, Merla sidled a bit closer while remaining on the bush. Fluffing out her shaggy neck feathers, she said, "Hungry, aren't you?"

Furious, Nashoba leaped at her. With ease, the raven fluttered out of reach to a nearby tree. *"Caw!"* she laughed. "And you're lame, too!"

Disgusted with himself and the bird, Nashoba lay on the ground, gasping for breath. Instead of looking at her, he studied his wounded foot. It was hurting. The scab had split, and blood was oozing. He turned to the bird. "For someone who knows everything," he said, "you ask a lot of questions."

"Ravens have a saying: Foolish creatures live by answers; wise creatures live by questions."

Nashoba, struggling again with his temper, snapped, "Are you going to tell me where the elk are or not?"

The raven shrugged, pointed her bill, and said, "Just beyond that knoll."

Nashoba turned quickly and looked. Thirty yards on, there was a rise in the ground, a knoll studded with gray boulders and close-standing trees. Taking a deep breath, he caught the distinct musty smell of elk.

He stood up. Ears pricked forward, he now heard the elks' slow puffy breathing. He heard calves squealing and mewing, the cows barking softly. He thought, *They must be grazing on new grass.*

Nashoba's momentary elation gave way to frustration that he had not found them on his own. All the same, he took a step toward the knoll.

"Stop!" the bird cried, with such urgency that Nashoba halted.

"Look here, wolf," she cried. "You're positively tottering. You're too old to catch anything by yourself."

"Must you insult me?" cried Nashoba.

"*Caw!* Here's another raven saying: an insult isn't an insult if it's the truth. If you go after those elk alone, you'll just frighten them away. If you want to be successful, you'll need to fetch your pack."

Sensing the bird was right, Nashoba clenched his jaws with annoyance. Then he said, "I don't want to lose the chance."

"Don't worry," said the raven. "We'll keep a watch."

"*We?*"

"Look up."

On the tree where Merla sat—but higher—seven ravens were perched on as many branches. They were gazing down at Nashoba, eyes bright like so many burning black candles.

"You call your family a *pack*," Merla said. "Do you know what humans call a group of ravens?"

"I don't care about humans."

"A *conspiracy* of ravens."

The wolf thought but did not say, *That's about right.*

"Listen to me, wolf," whispered the bird, "It's that time of year. *Everybody* in the forest is hungry. We ravens are just as hungry as you are.

"Very well," she continued. "Here's the offer. We guide you to the elk, and your pack will kill one, maybe two. Eat what you want. Just make sure you leave enough for us. That's the offer. Food for you, no trickery from us. Do you agree or not?"

Nashoba took his time before saying, "I agree."

"How smart of you," said the raven. "Now, get back to your pack and return quickly. To this exact spot. We'll keep an eye on the elk."

"It's miles," Nashoba said.

"Food, wolf, food."

Nashoba turned toward the knoll and sniffed again. The irksome bird was right. *Elk were there, no question.*

Next moment he began running back along the path he had just taken.

"Caw! Caw!" cried the raven. "Hurry, old wolf! Hurry!"

Ignoring the pain in his foot, and his weariness, Nashoba pushed himself to run faster.

That I have to depend on a bird! he thought. *Aggravating creature. A raven! The pack—especially Garby—will consider it a weakness. Well, no one need know. And if we get the elk, it won't matter. Yes, it will be a long run. Eight miles to the den. Eight miles back. But if the raven does keep a watch . . . then . . . no more starving!*

And I'll have shown Garby I'm not too old to hunt.

15

For Casey, the school day dragged. True, Fridays always seemed to last forever, with kids eager and impatient for the weekend. Fortunately, Friday recess was extra long. The school seemed to understand the kids' need to work off restless energy running and playing hard—not sitting.

Casey spent most of his time daydreaming about the "big gift" he was promised he would receive at dinner. He wanted so many things: the newest Madden football game, a new computer, airline tickets to visit his grandparents in Chicago, a bow-and-arrow set, cross-country skis, a dog. *What would he name a dog?*

He almost regretted that he and his mom had planned a party for Saturday afternoon, when he and a bunch of his friends—taken by his mom after her morning work—were going to a movie in Lockport, some seventeen miles on. At least he would have the morning to mess around with whatever the present was.

The picture of that zebra, feet up, which he had killed that morning, came into his mind. And the raven that had gotten away. *What*, he wondered, *would he kill when he got home?*

He could hardly wait.

16

As Nashoba hurried back to the den, he realized he should have investigated the elk for himself, considered the land to work out a hunting strategy, and decided which elk would be the easiest to take down. At the least, he should have counted them.

Yes, his wolves would follow him. However, with Gorby's challenge, they would be watching and judging everything he did. He must be successful.

The raven is right, he thought. *Elk cows often leave their calves alone. With any luck, the calves will not go far.*

Nashoba tried to run faster. He found it difficult. Twice he had to stop and rest, but the more he rested, the more anxious he became. He must not let those elk get away.

17

As the old wolf moved out of the valley, the hurt in his front paw worsened. Working hard to ignore it, he maintained a steady pace, the better to save his energy. When he came within a mile of the pack den, he stopped and rested. He did not want to appear tired when he arrived.

It was cooler at the higher altitude, a half-mile from the den. Tall lodgepole pine and spruce crowded the ground and shaded the dark green and fragrant air. The rocky earth was frozen in spots, often crusty with a brittle covering of dead leaves. Patches of dirty snow, dotted with pine needles, lay at random. Nothing new was growing here, not yet.

After sitting awhile to regain some strength—his right front leg elevated to ease the pain—Nashoba lifted his head, filled his lungs with air, closed his eyes, pointed his muzzle up, and made an O of his mouth. Then he howled a long deep wavering wail that lasted a good ten seconds. It rose and fell like a wave rolling across the sea. He was telling his pack of his return.

After a brief pause, Nashoba repeated the call once and once again. Before he was done, there were answering calls, five distinctive howls, each one in harmony with his voice.

His mate, Tonagan, had a higher-pitched call, full of excitement. Then came Garby's, loud and full of bluster. Nikito sang out too, tentative at first, then stronger as the young wolf asserted himself. Pildown added his voice—sweet and melodic. Finally Debalt, lowest in pack ranking—his short, almost barking howls sounded as if he were knocking on a door, asking to be let inside.

The soft-eared pups were too young to howl, but Nashoba had no doubt they heard his howls and were letting loose with excited squeaks and whines.

He gave a growl of satisfaction and resumed running faster now that he was close to home, paying no attention to his aching foot.

18

Casey's school day was over at three. The students at the school—there were only eighty-seven—either walked, were picked up in cars, or were taken home by school bus. But the bus did not go as far north as Casey's house. Instead Casey walked the short distance to the Clarksville General Store, where his mom worked.

The store was a long one-story wooden building with a central doorway. Two handwritten signs could be seen in a window. One read OPEN, the other, HUNTERS WELCOME HERE.

At one end of the building, groceries, meat, and vegetables were sold. An ice-cream counter did well during the summer tourist months. At the opposite end was a liquor store. Between this and the general store was the Clarksville Post Office.

Though the post office was only a small room

plus an adjacent hall, it served all North Rickles County. Since there was no delivery north of the post office, people came in for mail, news, and talk.

Next to the post office, which consisted of a large open counter, a cluttered workplace with desk, scales, postal sack racks, cash drawer, and safe, plus stamp drawers, was a wall of postal boxes. You opened your small box door with a brass key. There were also a few tables and chairs, plus a couple of shelves where you could exchange books, mostly paperbacks. Another wall was covered with local notices. There was a sign that read, CLARKSVILLE POST OFFICE—ESTABLISHED 1923.

"Hi, Mom!" Casey called as he approached.

His mother looked up from her desk and smiled. "How's my teenager?" She was wearing her blue post office shirt, on which she had embroidered *Postmaster—Clarksville* in red over her heart.

"I'm good."

"Go find yourself a snack. I know it's your birthday, but you might as well get some homework done. You've got a busy weekend," she added with another smile.

Casey replied with his own knowing grin.

19

When Nashoba reached the den, the wolves came forward to greet him in ranking order: Tonagan, Garby, Nikito, Pildown, and finally Debalt. They approached with tails respectfully low, then pushed their bodies against him with head and muzzle rubbing, as well as licking. While Garby avoided looking at Nashoba directly, Pildown dropped to the ground and whimpered. Debalt, as always, hung back, unsure he would be welcomed.

The two pups burst from the den. They yipped and yapped as they tumbled clumsily toward their father, tails wagging furiously. Though utterly disrespectful, Nashoba met their welcome with pleasure and no discipline, nuzzled them repeatedly, licked their faces, and nipped their soft ears. They responded by mouthing his jaw—again begging for meat—then plopped down, rolled on their backs, paws up, bellies exposed, all the while squealing with joy.

Tonagan looked on with satisfaction.

The wolves waited expectantly. Nashoba, wanting them to wait on him, took so much time that an impatient Garby burst out, "Well! Did you find anything?"

Nashoba looked at him disdainfully. "Of course," he said.

"Where? What?" asked Nikito with his usual enthusiasm.

Nashoba said, "A small herd of elk."

"How many?" demanded Garby.

"How far?" Nikito asked.

Nashoba chose to answer Nikito's question. "Down-valley. About eight miles."

"Eight?" said Tonagan.

"It will be dark before we reach them," said Garby.

"The moon will be good enough," Nashoba replied.

"If the weather holds," said Garby.

Nashoba ignored the challenge in the young wolf's remarks. "We'll go now. Debalt, you stay with the pups."

Proud to be given an important task, but disappointed not to be included in the hunt, Debalt lowered his head in obedience.

"Garby!" Nashoba commanded.

Garby approached cautiously.

Nashoba lifted his left paw and, in a sign of his authority, touched Garby's back. "Follow my lead," the old wolf said.

The young wolf kept his head down but made no response.

Nashoba turned and, despite his fatigue, began to run back the way he had come. Tonagan, as female leader, followed right behind. Garby came next. When the ever-eager Nikito drew too close to him, Garby looked back, showed his teeth, and snarled. Nikito fell back a step.

Hungry and excited, the pack ran in a line. Nashoba had to work hard to keep the lead.

20

Casey dumped his backpack on a chair and went to get a carton of milk from the fridge, as well as a package of small, chocolate-covered doughnuts from the grocery.

"Happy birthday, Case," called Mr. Pardella, the tall, skinny man with chin whiskers who tended the store's old-fashioned mechanical register. Everybody knew everybody in Clarksville.

"Thanks."

"Teenager, huh?"

"Guess."

"Here comes trouble!"

Casey laughed and returned to the table. When he got there, a man was standing at the post office counter talking to his mother while he mailed a small package. Casey recognized the man as Mr. Souza, an old white-haired guy who had come

to retire in the valley from some East Coast city. Casey did not know much about him, except that he was a "birder," someone who roamed the area looking for birds, taking pictures of them with a huge-lensed camera.

Once, Mr. Souza had come by their house asking permission to cross their land and go into the woods to look for birds. Since receiving an okay, he had often entered the forest from their place.

Casey was opening the doughnut package when he heard his mother say, "It can't be a wolf, Kim. Must have been a large dog."

Casey looked up.

"That's what I thought at first," said Mr. Souza. "But the paw prints were really big. I should have taken a picture. Back beyond your place, a half mile or so. Couple of weeks ago. I could have sworn they were wolf prints."

"I doubt it," Bess said. "Trust me, folks don't like wolves. Scared of them. If there was one that close, people would talk. Or worse."

"Well, I'm no expert, that's for sure," Mr. Souza said. "Did see lots of Cassin's finches back there.

Grosbeaks, too. Pretty birds. Oh yes, and some ravens."

Casey's mother told him the cost of his postage. "With priority mail," she said, "it should get to Boston in two, three days, latest."

"Thanks much," said Mr. Souza. As he passed Casey, he asked, "How's it going, Case?" but he did not stop.

"Fine."

Casey wanted to ask him about the paw prints. By the time he got up his nerve to do it and hurried out of the store, Mr. Souza was in his pickup truck and pulling out of the parking lot.

But it had begun to snow.

Casey did not care. Spring snow never lasted long. It might even turn to rain. All he could think was that wolves often appeared in his hunting game. It would be cool to see a real one.

✦ ✦ ✦

21

Snow was falling by the time the wolves came near the clearing. Nashoba, working against his exhaustion, was happy to halt.

"Wait here," he said. The four other wolves held back while Nashoba crept forward. Shivering, he stood behind a bush and peered out. His paw ached. His heart was beating so loudly, he wondered if the other wolves could hear it.

Ears cocked, eyes wide, nose sniffing, Nashoba studied the open area. The clammy air smelled of hard cold. Tiny snowflakes drifted down slowly, as if reluctant to drop. The ground was already layered with a thin veil of snow, which, in the fading dusk, seemed to glow. All was silent. There was no sign of the raven, or of elk.

Nashoba stole a quick look behind. The other wolves were watching him carefully. Tonagan's eyes were worried. Garby's were sullen. Nikito and Pildown stood patiently a few steps to the rear, their breath puffy and white.

Nashoba looked up. He could see no stars.

The old wolf turned back to the clearing, trying to decide what to do. *Where is that stupid raven? Should I wait for her? Should I try to find the elk on my own? They could be miles away by now, and this snow will make hunting much harder.*

22

"I was hoping we were done with snow," Casey's mom said as she headed north and home not long after five. She drove slowly, hands gripping the wheel. "Shouldn't have taken off the snow tires."

"Probably turn to rain," said Casey, barely looking up from his archery book. On his head he wore the camping head lamp he'd retrieved from the glove compartment. The lamp cast a circle of light on the page so he could read.

"How about calling your dad to see if it's snowing where he is?" his mom said. "We're still in cell-phone range." She took one hand off the steering wheel, quickly grabbed her purse from below, and flipped it toward Casey.

Casey rummaged through the purse, pulled out his mom's cell phone, and brought up his father's name. The phone rang ten times.

Finally his father's voice: "Hey there, teenager!"

Beaming, Casey said, "Hi. Where are you?"

"Still in Philbeck. More complicated than I thought. Just finishing up."

"Guess what?"

"What?"

"It's snowing."

"You're kidding! Raining here."

Casey turned toward his mom. "He's just finishing. No snow. Just rain."

She said, "Ask him when he'll be home."

"Mom wants to know—"

"You're breaking up!"

"When will you be home?" Casey said in a louder voice.

"Can't h—" The phone went dead.

"We're out of range." Casey put the phone back into his mom's purse.

"I do wish they'd put a cell tower up here. Be *so* much easier if we had service." She put on the car's headlights.

"I guess," said Casey, returning to his book.

His mom drove on, concentrating on the road. The wipers swished back and forth in a rhythmic beat. Casey glanced up. The driving snow looked like arrows coming right at them.

23

Nashoba took another quick glance back at his wolves. It was a mistake. He was sure they sensed his uncertainty. Mockery showed on Garby's face. Tonagan shifted uneasily.

"*Caw!*"

Coming from right overhead, the sound took Nashoba by surprise. Merla was perched on a tree branch, her blackness a hole in the falling snow, her beady eyes bright. Whether she had just landed—or had been there all along, watching him—Nashoba did not know.

"You *are* slow," said the bird.

"We're here, aren't we?" Nashoba snarled.

The raven cocked her head to one side. "I've decided you're actually twelve years old."

Nashoba felt deep hatred for the bird. How dare she talk to him this way? In front of the pack! *Had they heard?* It took all his willpower to stay. "Where are the elk?" he demanded.

Merla leaned forward, opened her beak, and stuck out her black tongue: a silent laugh.

"Tell me!" cried Nashoba.

"Are you truly ready?" the bird asked.

"I've a good mind to eat you," hissed the wolf.

"Feathers and all?"

"Even your bill."

"Thanks! I'll remember that. But *are* you ready, wolf?"

"Of course!" he cried, not daring to look back to see what the pack was making of this exchange.

"A quarter mile on, now," said the raven. "It should be quite easy for you all. *If* you do it right."

To Nashoba, the way she said "if" felt like a jab of her beak. "Just lead the way!" the wolf said with exasperation.

Merla fluffed her neck feathers, extended her wings, gave a *Caw!*, and leaped into the air.

Nashoba looked back. "Follow me!" he said to the wolves.

"As you follow a *bird*," Garby sneered.

Nashoba, pretending he had not heard, hurried after the raven. The other wolves fell in line, gray shadows in the milky white air.

24

It was almost six and rapidly growing dark when Casey and his mother drove up their dirt driveway.

The still-falling snow was two inches deep on their road. The SUV had no trouble getting through, though it lurched once to the right. Casey's mom, muttering, "Have to fill in that rut," made an instant adjustment. They were never in danger.

When they reached the house, she turned the car around. Casey jumped out and yanked up the garage door. A light went on automatically. A neat garage, its walls were hung with the family's skis, ski and fishing poles, snowshoes, a toboggan, and even a plow that could be mounted on the SUV. At the far end was a gun locker with two padlocks.

Casey's mom backed the SUV into the garage so the front end was pointing toward the road— a winter practice.

"I don't mind winter snow," Bess said, getting out of the car as Casey pulled down the door. "Expect it. But spring snow—that's Old Lady Nature making fun of us." She headed for the front door of the house.

"Spring snow *is* stupid," Casey agreed. He stopped to scoop up a snowball, and threw it at his mother's back, hitting her squarely.

"Thanks!" She laughed. "Hope your dad doesn't have any trouble. I forget: Did he take off his snow tires?"

"Don't think so."

"Good."

Once inside, Casey dropped his backpack in the mudroom. As his mother adjusted the house heat, she said, "I'll get dinner going."

"What are we having?"

"Your fave: roast chicken, fried potatoes, grilled carrots, and raspberry jam cake with vanilla icing. Thirteen candles," she added. "Plus one to grow on."

Casey made a thumbs-up sign then headed for his room and his computer game. In moments the arrow was aimed at the jungle, and he was waiting for animals to appear, ready to shoot them. He remembered the words in the archery book: *an arrow can be lethal when shot from a bow.*

I'm good, Casey told himself. *So good.*

25

Merla fluttered ahead, black wings flapping as she sprang—barely flying—from tree to tree. The light was growing dimmer, the snow still falling, but Nashoba never lost sight of her.

He noticed that seven other ravens were coming along, keeping to either side, like escorts. No squawks or calls, just the soft flutter of their wings. The pack wolves, equally hushed, stayed a few steps behind Nashoba.

The old wolf halted. From directly ahead, the musty smell of elk had reached him. The other wolves had also caught the scent. They stood by Nashoba's flanks, their breathing rapid with excitement, their whimpering sharp with hunger.

Merla landed on a branch directly in front of Nashoba. "*Now* do you smell them?" she asked, her voice low, full of scorn.

"Of course," Nashoba muttered.

"I've kept my part of the bargain," said the bird. "Now you need to keep yours. Make sure you leave enough for us."

Before Nashoba could reply, the raven flew up and disappeared. With a whisper of wings, the other ravens followed. The wolf wondered if they would stay near to watch the attack.

He looked around at his wolves. "Wait here," he said. "I need to see the elk."

"You didn't investigate them before, did you?" said Garby. "You're just taking orders from a bird."

Nashoba, ignoring the remark, trotted forward a few yards. Between the spot where he now stood and where the elk were was a thicket of oak brush and mountain shrub. There were aspen trees too, their slender trunks little more than rods of white in the clotted gloom. The air was streaked with bits of silent, sifting snow.

The old wolf listened intently. Now and again, the elk mewed, squealed, or made muted grunts and soft barks. Nashoba had no doubt they were grazing.

Knowing that elk had a keen sense of smell, he lifted his nose to get the direction of the wind. There was no movement. That was good. With luck, the elk would not smell them.

Lowering his body into a crouch, Nashoba inched forward.

The thicket was some twenty feet deep. Ground snow was sparse. Beneath the snow lay a thick brown matting of last fall's dead leaves, allowing Nashoba to step forward without a sound.

As he worked his careful way, he stepped on a small branch. It *snapped*. The old wolf froze, fearful that the elk had heard. When there was no reaction, he continued to creep forward.

Nearing the far side of the grove, he moved still slower and then stopped altogether. Only then did Nashoba realize that he had hunted this spot recently, but without success. This was where he had seen that white-haired human.

Hidden by trees and bushes, he stole a look.

He saw no humans, but he did see an elk cow standing like a sentry to one side of the small clearing. She was heavy and muscular, four feet tall at the tail, perhaps five hundred pounds in weight. Her reddish brown fur was shaggy, scruffy in spring molt. Her head and neck were held up and out, while warm, white breath puffed from her big nose. Pointed ears were pricked forward as she turned her head this way and that, alert for danger.

In the middle of the clearing stood five other cows, just as large as the sentry. They were pawing at the thin snow with their sharp, hard hooves, working to uncover new grass, then bending down to eat. Nashoba saw one calf, then four more. As the raven had told him, they were young, still spotted.

To Nashoba's eyes, it appeared as if the sentry cow had chosen her place because the clearing was small and surrounded by a circle of aspen. Though there were some gaps among the trees, the area was closed in, offering natural protection. All the same, Nashoba quickly perceived that if he and the wolves could block those gaps, the elk would be trapped, as if in a cage. How easy then to kill a calf or two. Even better, if the wolves moved fast enough and the elk panicked, the pack might bring down a cow.

One of the calves moved toward a cow—*its mother*, Nashoba supposed. The calf looked to weigh forty, maybe fifty pounds. As it moved, it limped. Something was wrong with its rear left leg. That meant the calf would not be able to move as fast as the others, making it an even easier target.

The young elk began to nurse.

Nashoba's decision was instantaneous: he would go after the hobbled calf. The thought of eating made his stomach growl.

Turning, he stole back to the pack, moving as quickly as he dared.

26

Casey's mom looked into his room. "Guess your dad has had some road trouble. Dinner will be late, love."

"I'm good," said Casey, not even turning her way. Instead he sat in front of his computer, the Bowhunter game bright on the screen. As before, it showed a jungle scene whose lush colors reminded Casey of an animated movie about summer. Thinking of the snow outside, he had to smile. *No jungle here.*

At the bottom of the screen, the arrow shaft and arrowhead pointed toward the jungle. Casey shifted his mouse so that the arrow aimed now this way, then that.

He clicked the *W* button on his keyboard. The jungle began to move, as if he, Casey, were walking deeper and deeper into it. He kept his hand hovering over the mouse, waiting for an animal to appear.

A wolf sprang into view.

Casey clicked his mouse. The arrow shot forward, unspooling its red course like a bloody ribbon. The wolf made a sudden turn, avoiding the arrow, and bounded off.

Bad shot! said the automated voice. *Try again. Be alert! Aim better!*

Determined to improve, Casey stared at the screen, flexing the fingers of his right hand over the mouse. The jungle rolled toward him.

The way the game worked, an animal who

escaped being killed *always* came back. During every half hour of play all the animals he killed returned. He was waiting for the wolf to come back.

In the Bowhunter game there was no death, just kills.

27

"Six cows, four calves," Nashoba whispered to the four waiting wolves. "In a small clearing surrounded by trees. One of the cows is standing sentry on the left side. There are a few gaps among the trees—bolt-holes. There's no wind.

"Garby, you go to the left, behind that sentry. Block her. Tonagan, you go to the right. Nikito, you need to get around to the far side and go forward. Pildown, you'll stay behind me and back me up. If we can do that, we should have them trapped."

"And you?" asked Garby.

"There's a lame calf," Nashoba continued in a low

voice. "I'll get that one. Does everyone understand? I'll make the first move. The rest of you will wait for me, then do what you can. We should do well.

"Now, get into place. Nikito, you have the farthest to go. I'll hold back until I'm sure you're there. Remember," he said, "*only* when I break from the tree cover to attack will you attack. Not before."

"Don't worry," Garby said. "I'll bring down that sentry cow."

Nashoba glared at him. "Just let me get to that calf first," he snapped. "If we bring down more, fine. Is that understood?"

Garby gave a tiny nod.

Wanting to ease the tension, Nashoba said, "Of course, the more we get, the better for all. Are we ready?"

There were grunts of agreement.

"Food, my friends," said Nashoba. "Food is close."

28

Casey's dad did not get home until seven thirty. The boy was still at the computer. His kill score had reached forty-nine. Only the wolf had eluded him.

"I'm home!" Casey heard, along with the stomping of boots in the mudroom.

Within moments his dad poked his head into Casey's room. "Sorry," he said. "The road's really slick. Can't believe it will come down for long. Your mom says dinner's ready."

Casey jumped up.

To his surprise, the dining room, which the family seldom used, had sprouted colored streamers, even dangling letters that read HAPPY BIRTHDAY!

A conical birthday hat sat near each plate.

"Hats?" said a laughing Casey. "You kidding? I'm too old."

"You only become a teenager once," Bess replied with a laugh of her own.

"Happy birthday, Son!"

Casey's eyes were on the big long white box that lay across his chair.

"Can I open it?" asked Casey.

"Might be fun," said his dad.

In a matter of seconds Casey had ripped the box open.

Inside was a simple but elegant wooden bow, as graceful as a sculpture. Almost four feet long, its upper and lower limbs were equal in length and curvature, the bowstring designed to reach from matching notches at the tips of the recurve. The bow's central riser was laminated wood.

"Oh my God!" Casey exclaimed. "Fantastic."

"There are many different kinds of bows," his dad explained. "But yours is called a longbow. Twenty-pound draw."

"Awesome!" said Casey, sliding a hand along the bow's smooth length.

"When you're not using it, you're supposed to keep it unstrung," his mom said. "Like a trigger lock on a gun. Safety first."

"There's a bowstringer in the box," his dad

pointed out. "String, arrows, arm guard, plus some paper targets. Everything you need."

"Thanks!" Casey cried, holding the bow now this way, then that way. "I love it! Thanks. Thanks so much!"

His parents grinned at his pleasure.

"We'll work with you to set it up," said his dad.

"But it is a weapon," his mother added. "So we found someone to give you skill and safety lessons. You need to learn both. Tim Fowler from town. Starting next weekend."

"Great," Casey said, and reached into the box to pull out six white arrows.

"Called composite arrows," said his dad. "A mix of aluminum and carbon. Considered the best. Being white, they should be easy to find in the forest."

Casey touched the tips and looked up. "Sharp," he said.

"That's the whole point," said his mom.

Though it was a bad pun, they all laughed.

"Can I hunt with it?" Casey asked.

"It's what the lessons are for," his mom said.

"Hey, archery hunting season begins September first. You'll be ready."

"But we can start fiddling around in the morning," said his dad.

Casey turned to his mother. "Did you tell Dad what that Mr. Souza said?"

"Who?"

"Kim Souza. That old guy. The birder. Said he saw wolf tracks back behind our place."

"Not likely," said Casey's dad. "Wolves up in Wyoming. Sure. But not here. Though I suppose they could have drifted down."

Casey said, "They're killers, right?"

"Unless they're sick with something like rabies, wolves don't attack people. Elk, deer, sheep, and cattle: that's a completely different story. But no, not humans. They avoid people. Still, I wouldn't mess with a wolf."

✧ ✧ ✧

29

Nashoba waited as three of the wolves moved toward their positions. Pildown remained. Nashoba touched his nose to his muzzle by way of encouragement, then turned back into the aspen grove. He moved forward noiselessly, placing his feet with great care. All the while, he kept his eyes straight ahead, watching, ears cocked forward, listening.

Pildown followed, stiff-tailed.

Nashoba knew that Nikito, with the farthest to go, would take the longest time to get into place. That placement was the most crucial, because it would be exactly opposite his own position of attack. The moment Nashoba showed himself, the elk would bolt straight away from him. When they saw Nikito blocking their way, they would panic. That panic would give the other wolves their best opportunity. First, however, it was up to him, as pack leader, to commence the attack with a successful kill of that limping calf.

Nashoba reached the clearing edge. With no moon or starlight, it was only ground snow that provided a pale glimmering. All else was shadowy. The grazing cows were pawing the ground, their breathing hardly more than little popping puffs.

Nashoba looked for his target calf. The young elk was on the ground, legs folded under, near a cow. He might even be asleep. *Better yet*, Nashoba thought. Every second helped.

Fleetingly he glanced up among the surrounding trees and saw the glint of raven eyes. The eight birds were deep among the dark branches, still as stone, watching, waiting.

Nashoba checked the sentry elk. She was where she had been, but her movements had become agitated, suggesting she had become suspicious.

The old wolf looked across the clearing, hoping to catch some glimmer of Nikito. He saw none.

He turned back to the sentry. The cow gave a sharp snort. The other cows paused in their feeding, looked up and around. *They are nervous.* Nashoba looked for the cause.

He caught the gleam of Garby's eyes. The young wolf had slipped among the trees, behind the sentry cow. But instead of waiting, he was creeping forward, preparing to strike first.

Don't! barked Nashoba in his head. *Don't!*

The sentry cow jerked her head around and snorted. She appeared to look straight at Garby.

Don't show yourself! Nashoba cried out in his thoughts. *Don't show yourself!*

He turned back to his target calf. Even as he spotted her, the calf awoke and jumped up.

The next moment the sentry cow gave a sharp *bark!*—the elks' alarm signal. She must have seen Garby. Her call brought an explosion of sounds from the elk—squealing, barking. Simultaneously they rushed toward the trees.

Knowing he must attack, Nashoba—front legs pumping in unison—sprang into the clearing, hurling himself at the calf, which stood frozen in terror. But the wolf's right front paw—the hurt one—buckled slightly, breaking his charge.

Though he knew he was not close enough—more than five feet from the calf—Nashoba leaped, jaws wide, teeth exposed, aiming for the calf's haunches. Even as he committed himself, the calf's mother whirled about, shoved her calf to one side, and kicked out with a rear leg. The kick smashed into Nashoba's right shoulder, powerful enough to break his leap. He fell short, crashing to the earth. The cow and her calf burst toward the trees.

On the ground, Nashoba heard sounds of hoofbeats, frantic elk barking, snarls and grunts from the wolves. All the old wolf could feel was the shock of terrible pain. He tried to move. He could not. The pain engulfed him. The next moment his mind went dark, darker than the night.

30

Casey lay on his bed reading *Archery Fundamentals*, his new bow on the floor by his side. He and his dad had strung and restrung it a number of times, so Casey could now do it himself.

His book was open to the section titled "Finding Your Dominant Eye." After much testing, Casey decided his right eye was it. That eye, according to the book, should be the one closest to the bow-string when he shot an arrow.

Then Casey went over the nine steps for a perfect shot.

Take your stance
Nock the arrow
Set your grip
Predraw your bow
Draw your bow
Anchor
Aim
Release
Follow-through

His dad promised that in the morning they would set up a target for practice and work on all those steps.

His mother looked into the room. "Hey, love: Toby Manhock's mother just called. Said the weather is bad enough that he can't come tomorrow."

"Oh," said Casey, fully absorbed in his book.

"I'm thinking," his mother said, "maybe we should postpone the party for a week. Snow will absolutely be gone by then. What do you say?"

Casey looked up. A delayed party would mean a whole day to practice with the bow. He said, "Fine with me."

"Sure?"

"Sure."

"I'll make the calls," his mom said, and retreated.

Casey looked down at the bow, its smooth wooden surface, and its graceful curves. He had never seen anything so beautiful. Tomorrow he would use it.

31

Nashoba could not tell where the pain in his body began nor where it ended. He kept trying to move but could not. He worked to open his eyes but failed. He was not sure where he was or how much time was passing. All that he felt was pain, a universe of hurt, and he was the center of it.

Then someone was licking his muzzle. Sensing another lick, he struggled to open his eyes, and managed a squint. Tonagan was standing over him, bending so close, he could feel her breath on his eyes. She licked him again.

Nashoba lifted his head a few inches off the ground and realized that the other wolves were standing around him, watching.

"How . . . how did we do?" he managed to ask.

Tonagan said, "They all got away."

"*All . . . ?*"

"All."

"*Nothing* taken?"

No reply. It was answer enough.

The effort to speak drained Nashoba of energy. He closed his eyes and lowered his head to the earth. He breathed deeply.

"It was a bad plan," said a voice. Nashoba knew it was Garby. The old wolf wanted to curl his lips in disgust and show his teeth. The gesture was beyond him.

"You're too old, Nashoba," called Garby. "Useless. You let a stupid cow knock you down."

Nashoba waited a few moments, gathered some strength, and replied, "I ordered you . . . to wait for me before attacking."

"The pack should attack with strength, not weakness," Garby returned.

Nashoba let the words settle. Then he said, "What happened?"

"When you failed," said Garby, "it threw everything into confusion. They were able to get away."

"So you, too, got nothing," said Nashoba.

"Because *you* failed," snapped Garby.

Pain prevented Nashoba from responding.

"But from now on," Garby continued, "we'll have strength to lead us. I am the pack leader now."

Nashoba peeked up into Tonagan's face. He saw his hurt reflected in her eyes. Full of anger, the old wolf pushed down with his front legs so he could stand and confront Garby. The effort brought agony. Collapsing, he lay on the ground, panting.

"Give up, Nashoba," said Garby. "You can't do anything."

As the wolves lingered, Nashoba had a thought: *Are they waiting for me to die?*

He lifted his head again. "Is that what you all want?" he whispered. "You want Garby to lead?"

Pildown spoke gently. "Nashoba, we must find food."

"I can still hunt," the old wolf said.

"No, you can't," said Garby.

"I have one more kill in me," Nashoba said, managing with great effort to look right at Garby.

"Try," said the young wolf, and he drew close.

Nashoba attempted to clear his mind of the

hatred he felt toward Garby. He could not. All he said was, "Go away. All of you."

None of the wolves moved.

Nashoba lifted his head a few inches. "Go!" he barked in a burst of breath. "Leave me alone!" He rested his snout on the snow-covered ground between his two large front paws, and breathed deeply.

Nashoba heard the wolves move away. He sensed that only Tonagan remained. She pressed her nose into his ear while making a small whining sound. "I'll come back," she said.

"Go," whispered Nashoba, not even looking at her.

"Tonagan!" barked Garby. "Hurry. We need to go after those elk."

Nashoba made no effort to watch them leave. Instead he stared at the snow right before him. It was pink, stained with his own blood.

Blowing snow tickled his eyes, causing him to blink. He gave a deep sigh. The pain in his leg pulsed with the beating of his heart. All he wanted was sleep.

32

In the middle of the night Casey woke to the ringing of the house phone. He assumed, because it happened with some regularity, that his father was being called for a power problem. He eyed his digital clock: 3:20 in bloodred numbers.

Half awake, half asleep, Casey listened to his dad's voice but couldn't make out his words. He did hear his mother calling, "Be safe!"

Casey listened to his father's truck rumble and then, within moments, heard the diminishing sound of it crunching down the dirt road.

The silence returned.

Casey rolled from bed, raised the blinds, and looked out the window. Only a few flakes of snow were falling. High in the sky hung a crescent moon. Streaks of dark clouds moved slowly across its pale yellow face. The moonglow was bright enough to cast long purple shadows—like reaching fingers—across the silvery snow.

Thinking *It's going to be a good day for hunting*, Casey went back to bed—forgetting to pull the blinds down—and quickly fell asleep.

33

Flakes of cold snow fell on Nashoba's face and brought him back to the world. He heard the flap of wings. It took him some moments to grasp that Merla was standing before him. Hearing more fluttering, he supposed the other ravens had gathered and were looking down at him.

"Is he dying?" he heard one ask.

"Could be," Merla replied.

"How long will it take?" asked another.

"Don't know," said Merla.

Nashoba assumed they were waiting so they

could feast on him. Ravens, which lived on dead things, always started with the eyes.

Nashoba squeezed his shut.

Wondering if he would ever awaken, he slept.

34

"Caw!"

A sharp poke in the nose woke Nashoba. Through barely open eyes he became aware that there was early morning light.

"Wolf!" came a cry, and another peck. "Are you alive?"

Nashoba focused and saw Merla standing before him at eye level, her head cocked slightly to one side. She was observing him. In the pure white of the surrounding snow her blackness was absolute, her ebony eyes fierce. She was about to peck Nashoba again, when she saw his eyes were open.

"Ah!" the raven exclaimed. "Not dead!"

"Not yet," Nashoba rumbled, aware now that his entire body hurt—a misery of pain, stiffness, and weakness.

"But not *very* alive," said the raven, bobbing her head.

Nashoba opened his eyes wider but quickly closed them against the glare of the glistening snow. "How long have I been here?" he asked, his eyes slits.

"All night," said Merla. "Sun's up. Snow stopped. Blue skies. Might be a fine day. Unless it rains. Don't you think?"

Nashoba said nothing.

He sensed that he was lying in inches of snow. He did not care. He opened his mouth wide and yawned. He moved his ears, neck, and tail. Finally he tried to move his legs, one at a time, starting from the rear. Everything seemed to work except his right front leg and paw. The pain was extreme from the shoulder down.

For some moments he lay quietly, becoming aware that he was terribly thirsty. Leaning forward, he stuck out his tongue and lapped the snow before him. It was good, but not enough.

Merla watched him with interest. "Do you want me to tell you what happened?" she asked.

"No," said the wolf.

Ignoring him, the raven said, "A complete bungle." Once again she bobbed her head in self-agreement.

"I need water," said the wolf.

"There's a creek not far. Can you stand?"

Nashoba had to think about it. Then he made the effort the way he always did, by pushing down with his front legs. He rose a few inches, but the pain was so intense, he dropped down quickly.

"Try again," said the raven.

Resting a moment to let the hurt subside, Nashoba thought about what he might do, could do. Taking a deep breath, he pressed upward with his rear legs, lifting his rump first. Then he shoved down using only his left front leg. Despite the searing pain, he started to rise, managing to get about six inches off the ground, then lost his balance and fell.

"I can't stand," he said, and gasped.

"*Caw!*" cried the raven. "You *are* a mess!"

Nashoba stayed still for a few long moments,

breathing deeply. Telling himself there was no way to avoid pain, that he had to accept it, he made another effort to stand. He fell again.

"Pretty pathetic," said Merla.

"Haven't you anything better to say?" Nashoba muttered.

"I always tell the truth."

"I don't want to hear it!" cried the wolf.

"*Caw!*" answered the raven. "Creatures never want the truth about themselves, only others."

"You are boring," said Nashoba.

"Wisdom is always boring," taunted the raven. "That's why no one listens to it."

Nashoba said nothing.

Merla remained in place, watching him.

After a while Nashoba said, "I need water."

"Here," said the bird. With that, she squatted, spread her wide black wings, and swept snow into the wolf's face. Startled, Nashoba pulled back, only to realize what the bird had done. There was now a pile of snow before his nose. He stretched out his snout and lapped it up.

Then he said, "And something to eat."

The raven bobbed her head a third time. "You're very demanding," she said.

Nashoba grunted.

"Be right back," said Merla. "Don't go anywhere!" With that, she spread her wings and flew away.

Nashoba, wondering at the bird's sense of humor, had no idea where she was going.

35

The morning's bright sunlight streamed through the window and woke Casey. For a few moments he remained unmoving, enjoying being in bed. Then he checked his digital clock. It was almost seven. He got up and looked out the window.

Snow covered the ground. On pine branches, sagging gobs of it looked like melting vanilla ice cream. A slight breeze caused snowflakes to rise from the ground and float through the air. Illuminated by the low sun, the snow bits sparkled like tiny diamonds. It was what his mom called "a glitter morning."

Hearing someone moving around the house, Casey went to the kitchen. His mother was at the counter, having a cup of coffee and some toast with honey. She looked up. "Morning, love."

"Dad back?"

"You hear him take off?"

"Where'd he have to go?"

"Some transformer problem over by Albers. Stupid snow. Botched the whole network. But look," she said, gesturing to the window. "A nice day."

Casey, thinking of the promised time with his new bow and arrow, said, "He going to be back soon?"

She shrugged. "You know. Gets back when he gets back. Then the two of you can work with your bow. Anyway, I have to leave for work. Sorry about your birthday party." She glanced out a window. "Shouldn't have canceled."

"It's okay," he said, thinking of the bow.

She stood up. "Hungry? Some muffins left. Help yourself. I'll be back no later than two thirty. Want to come with me, or stay?"

Casey shrugged. "I'll stay."

"No saying when Dad will get back."

"I don't mind being alone."

"Okay. I'll get dressed."

Casey went to his computer, clicked on Bow-hunter, and began the game. *Good practice*, he told himself.

36

Nashoba's pain so blotted away his sense of time, he had no idea how long the raven was gone. When she finally reappeared, it seemed to him as if she had only just left.

Holding something in her beak, she walked up to Nashoba and dropped her offering in front of him. "Food," she announced.

The wolf sniffed. It was revolting. "What is it?" he asked, nose wrinkling.

"Rabbit."

Nashoba sniffed again. "It's rotten," he said with disgust.

"What do you care?" squawked the raven. "When was the last time you ate? It's food, wolf."

"Where did it come from?"

"Considering your situation, you're particular. If you must know, it's something I cached."

"How long ago?"

"Never mind when. It's what I'm offering. And you want food."

Nashoba, who liked his meat as fresh as possible, felt offended. He looked away. As moments passed, despite the body ache, he could not ignore the hunger pangs. Stretching out his head, trying to keep from gagging, he took the food into his mouth. His impulse was to spit it out, but he swallowed it down. It tasted as bad as it smelled.

"Was that good?" asked the raven.

"Awful," said the wolf.

"Then you don't want me to fetch you anything else?"

It took a moment for the wolf to say, "Something better?"

"Probably not," squawked the raven.

"Then why are you offering?" asked Nashoba.

The raven fluffed out her feathers. "Do you know what would happen if I didn't bring you food?"

"Nothing," said the wolf.

"Nothing?" screamed the bird. "You'd die."

"Why should you care?"

The raven pulled back her head and stared at Nashoba. Then she nodded vigorously. "Let me tell you something, wolf," she cried. "You are a stupid, helpless creature! You are incapable of taking care of yourself. You are *exactly* what that young wolf from your pack said: old and useless."

Humiliated, Nashoba said nothing.

"And don't tell me you're merely hurt," added the bird. "You are not just old—you're stuffed with vanity and pride." She bobbed her head again in agreement with herself.

"And you are a conceited bully," the wolf muttered.

"I have a lot to be conceited about," the raven threw back. "I'm healthy, smart, and I, at least, am capable of taking care of myself. I intend to live forever."

Nashoba, truly baffled, said, "Why are you helping me?"

"Because I'm old too, you fool! Older than you. Most ravens live to be thirteen. I'm twelve. Do you think anyone *young* would understand you? Do you think young ones care about old ones? Or would take pity on us? *Caw!*" Merla hopped right up to Nashoba's nose and gave him a small peck. "If this old bird doesn't take care of you," she clacked, "no one will!"

Merla backed away and ruffled her shaggy neck feathers. "Besides, I led you into this. I should have known better. From the moment I saw you, you were a limping, bedraggled, and starving old beast. *Caw!* There's nothing more foolish than when one fool helps another fool. Pitiful!" She bobbed her head. "I speak for myself, of course. And you."

Nashoba shut his eyes.

"My point, exactly," said the bird. "You hear the truth, and all you can do is shut me out."

"Leave me alone," said Nashoba.

"No! I may eat you when you're dead, but I won't kill you. Raven's honor! "

"Horrible!" Nashoba cried.

"Doesn't make it less true," Merla said. "Do you have pups?"

"Yes."

"How old?"

"They're mouthing me for real food."

"Want some advice?"

"No."

"Take care of them. Let them grow old. Old enough to remember when they ignored their old father."

The wolf made no reply.

"How many years were you leader of your pack?"

"Six."

"What happened to the old leader?"

"She died."

"How?"

"It was far north of here. She was going after some cattle. A human killed her."

Merla stared at him. "I suppose I need to tell you, we're not that far from humans right now."

Unease filled Nashoba. "Do you know where they live?"

The raven looked up and around, then pointed with her beak. "In that direction."

"Will they come here?"

"Not likely." The raven bobbed her head. "I'll get you something more to eat." She stretched her wings, gave a loud *caw!,* and flew off.

Nashoba watched her go, trying to make sense of what the bird had said. "*She* is the fool," he said aloud.

All the same, Merla's mention of humans added to his wretchedness. He felt abandoned.

The wolf lay quietly for a few moments then decided he must try again to get up. If he could just make his way back to the den . . . He'd let Garby be pack leader. He'd take Debalt's position—at the bottom. At least he would be part of a pack.

Taking a deep breath, Nashoba began to rise as before, by shoving up his rump. Then, using all his remaining strength, his whole body trembling, Nashoba rose on his left front leg. Briefly—a little longer than before—he remained standing until his body began to shake. Dizziness came. The next moment he tumbled sideways onto his bad shoulder. The pain exploded.

Panting, Nashoba lay where he had fallen. He was waiting, but what he was waiting for, he had no idea. *Maybe the raven is right,* he thought. *Maybe Garby is right. Maybe I am a fool. Maybe it would be better if I died.*

The old wolf closed his eyes. The darkness was light enough.

37

Shielding his eyes against the glare of the melting snow, Casey watched his mother drive out of the garage and go carefully down the dirt road. When he lifted a hand to wave good-bye, she gave two beeps of her horn. The next moment she was out of sight.

Casey stooped over, grabbed two fistfuls of snow,

squeezed them into a ball, and threw it at nothing in particular. Then he returned to the house, leaving the garage door open for his mother's return.

Inside, he turned back to Bowhunter, only to tell himself he did not have to play a game. He could use his real bow. It was right there by the side of his bed.

Casey picked it up and admired the fine wood again, its lovely curves, its sweet balance. Smiling, he recalled what he had read in that book, how powerful a bow and arrow could be. How powerful *he* could be.

He took up his bowstringer—a long, thick cord with leather pockets at either end. As he had practiced with his dad, he looped the larger leather pocket over one bow tip, and then fitted the second pocket on the other end. Holding the bow in the middle with this left hand, putting his foot down on the bow stringer, he pulled up. The action bent the bow enough for him use his free hand to fit the bowstring itself on the two bow tips.

Once he had checked that the string was properly attached, he lowered the bow. The bowstringer slipped off, but the real bowstring remained, taut and strong. He plucked it. It made a lovely twang. The bow was ready. He was ready.

He nocked an arrow on the string. He was about to give a pull, when the words about safety his parents had spoken came into his head. He needed to go outside.

Bow in one hand, arrows in the other, Casey stood in front of his house and tried to recall all nine steps he was supposed to take for every shot.

Impatient to try, he could remember only three of the steps. One: take the proper stance. Two: nock the arrow. Seven: aim.

What would he shoot at? He looked around. He decided that the garage would be the best target. It was big, and the door was open. He would shoot the arrow inside so he would be able to find it.

He selected one, dropping the others to the ground. After nocking his arrow, Casey took a wide stance, pulled back the arrow and string, used his right eye to aim, and released the arrow. *Twang!*

Instead of going straight, the arrow flew wildly high, hit the garage roof at an angle, caromed off, and kept going, disappearing among the trees beyond.

Casey stood stock-still, astonished that the shot had gone so crazily. His parents would be upset if he lost that arrow. *He* was upset.

Not wanting to lose the arrow, he set off through the snow in the direction he was sure the arrow had flown—toward the trees.

In one hand, he clutched the bow. In the other, he held the remaining arrows.

38

Nashoba awoke, uncertain where he was. His whole body ached. He was terribly stiff. His paw and shoulder hurt. The urine stench was strong. He was, he realized with dismay, lying in his own puddle.

He looked about with bleary eyes, but the surroundings seemed unfamiliar. Where was Tonagan?

The pups? The other wolves? Only gradually did he recall all that had happened.

Where was the raven? Would she come back? He worried that she was insulted. He should not have argued with her. Yes, a raven was an unusual friend for a wolf, but she was a friend nonetheless. Now she was the only one he had. She, at least, was helping him.

He shut his eyes and dozed. He dreamed he was young and running through the forest, Tonagan by his side. The pups were scrambling to keep up. The other wolves in the pack trotted behind him, tails wagging. Then the dream changed, and the pups were mouthing his muzzle, the young begging for life.

"*Caw!*"

Nashoba blinked his eyes open to see Merla holding a dead mouse in her beak. She hopped forward.

"How old is *that*?" Nashoba asked.

The raven dropped the shriveled carcass. "What difference does it make? It's food. And it's younger than you." Using her beak, she pushed the dead mouse closer to the wolf. He sniffed, hesitant.

"It'll keep you alive," the raven coaxed.

Nashoba braced himself and then, nauseating as it was, ate the mouse.

"Do you think," asked Merla, "any of your pack will return for you?"

"I told them to leave me alone."

Merla cocked her head. "Do you want to know another raven saying?"

"No."

"*Caw!* The bigger you think you are, the smaller you are."

"You tire me," said the old wolf.

"Actually," said Merla, "I'm saving you. Let me see what else I can find." She flew off.

Nashoba, feeling great urgency to get away, to get back to his pack, once again tried to move, but failed. He wondered if he would ever move again, if he would spend the rest of his life—a shortened life, surely—listening to the raven tell him what an old and useless creature he was.

39

Casey could not find the arrow. He looked back, trying to retrace in his mind the path the arrow had taken from the garage roof. He tried to think it through like a geometry problem. What was the angle of its flight? Its vectors.

He looked up. The sky was clouding over. The air was warmer and smelled of rain. He marveled at how changeable spring weather could be.

He walked to the right, and then to the left, recalling that expression he had heard: *finding a needle in a haystack*. In this case, it was a white arrow in a melting snowfield.

The Setons' open land extended some thirty yards beyond their house. After that stood trees marking the boundary to the national forest. It went on for miles, reaching into higher country.

Casey saw that there was less snow on the

ground under the trees than where he stood in the open. Was it possible that the arrow went that far? He scolded himself: *I never should have shot the arrow. Where was I wrong? My grip? My fingers? I didn't hold the arrow the way the book said I should.*

He listened intently as if he might hear where the arrow had landed.

"*Caw!*"

Was that a crow? A raven? Casey scanned the wall of trees. At first he saw nothing. Only after a few moments of searching did he spot something big and black high in a lodgepole pine. He thought it was just a shadow. It took him a few moments to see that it was a bird sitting on a branch, and the bird seemed to be looking right at him. *A raven,* Casey figured, from the size of it. *Smart birds,* he told himself. The sight of the raven reminded him of Bowhunter.

Moving slowly so as not to startle the bird, Casey put his arrows on the ground, picked out one of the five, and nocked it on the string. He hefted the bow, took a stance, recalling the right way to hold the arrow in the string this time, and aimed it at the bird.

With a loud *"Caw!"* the raven leaped into the air, swerved about, and flew deeper into the forest.

Casey lowered his bow. *So like my game,* he thought. Feeling challenged, he bent over, picked up his arrows, and began to follow the raven, now his target.

40

Merla landed right in front of Nashoba. "Wake up!" she screamed.

Nashoba opened his eyes. "Did you bring more of your awful food?"

"A human is coming this way," she cried.

"Here?" said a startled Nashoba.

Merla bobbed her head rapidly. "This direction."

A jolt of panic swept through the wolf. "Is . . . is he coming after me?"

"I have no idea. But he's coming."

Nashoba turned his head first one way and then another, but saw no sign of any human. Only when he sniffed did human scent reach him.

"I smell him," he whispered. Fearful, he looked at Merla. "Is he trying to kill me?"

"He has *something* in his hands," answered the bird. "I'm not sure what it is, but I've seen it before. I'm pretty sure it can kill."

Bird and wolf stared at each other.

Nashoba said, "I have one more kill in me."

"You do not!" cried Merla. "You can't even move!"

Nashoba made no answer. Instead he fought to gain some sense of his whole body—what would work, what would not.

He pushed down with his rear legs. His rump came up. Knowing he had no choice but to endure the pain, he pushed down with his front paws, stressing the left side.

He stood.

Merla hopped back, bobbing her head with encouragement.

Though he was standing, Nashoba felt miserable.

When the forest seemed to spin around him and his body swayed, he closed his eyes. *Don't fall, don't fall, don't fall.*

He opened his eyes again. To his enormous relief he was still upright.

"Good!" cried Merla. "Stay still. Gather yourself. Gather your strength."

Nashoba struggled to find enough energy.

Merla asked, "Feel better? Stronger?"

"A little."

"Now," said the raven, "try walking. Even a small step will be good. Lead with your left leg. Easy on the right!"

The best Nashoba could do was hop his left leg forward a few inches. Trembling from nose to tail, he wobbled.

"Any movement is better than none!" Merla cried.

The wolf looked at the matted snow where he had been lying. There was blood, urine, and scat. He felt revulsion at himself.

Clenching his teeth, he took another left-leg hop toward Merla—who had jumped out of the way—

and hauled the rest of himself along in the same direction. The effort worked. A bit. Moreover, the movement gave him some confidence.

"I can walk," he said, proud of his small achievement but embarrassed that he should feel so.

"A little," returned the bird.

"Where should I go?" Even as Nashoba asked the question, he realized he was leaving all decisions to the raven.

"Anywhere, as long as it's away from that human," she replied.

"I don't know how far I can manage."

"Doesn't matter!" shrieked Merla. "Wherever you get will be better than here."

Nashoba took another hop and step forward.

"Fine! Good!" the raven cried. "Keep it up. I'll go back and try to distract that human."

"Don't put yourself in danger."

"I'm small."

Nashoba grunted. "There's an old wolf expression: the smaller you think you are, the bigger you are."

Merla opened her beak and stuck out her tongue. "Glad you listened."

She flew off.

Nashoba watched her swoop among the trees until she was lost to view. *A good friend,* he told himself.

He turned and took another step. *How far,* he wondered, *will I need to go to be safe?*

How far *could* he go?

He glanced upward. Seven ravens were perched on the trees, looking down at him.

They're still waiting for me to die, Nashoba thought.

41

Casey stood among the trees, searching for the bird. If he could shoot it, he would feel a lot less dumb about the arrow he had lost. Standing there, determined not to mess up a second time, he again made himself try to review all nine points of bow shooting in the archery book.

"Caw! Caw!"

Casey spun about and spotted the raven high in a tree—not where he had expected.

It really was just like the video game.

He took his stand. Nocked an arrow. Set his grip.

The next moment, the bird flew off, but not so far as to be out of sight. "I thought it was smart," Casey murmured. "Birds in the game are smarter."

Relaxing his grip, he scooped up his arrows. Then he moved toward the bird, determined to get a shot.

42

Nashoba took fourteen more hop-steps. The effort exhausted him. His whole body quivered. The agony was great. Worst of all, he was aware that he had gone only a small way.

I can't go anymore, he told himself, and slumped to the ground. Breathless, he lay in the melting snow. Not knowing what else to do, he reached out and licked his wounded paw.

Hearing a soft *pit-pat, pit-pat*, he looked around. It had begun to rain, the drops barely reaching him through the trees. From a distance thunder rumbled. When he looked up, he saw that the watching ravens had flown away.

Is that a good sign or a bad one?

From a distance he heard, *"Caw!" Where,* he wondered, *is Merla?* Had she managed to lead the human away?

When she came back, he must tell her how grateful he was.

43

Twice, Casey had come in to what he thought would be good shooting range. Both times—at the last moment—the bird had flown in an unexpected direction.

Maybe she's not so dumb, he told himself, enjoying the hunt, ignoring the steady, light rain. From far off, there was a flash of lightning. Seven seconds later soft thunder came.

Following the raven's changeable flight path, Casey moved deeper into the forest. Every now and then he paused to check his surroundings. He knew the woods well enough to know where he was.

When the bird eluded him yet again, Casey began to wonder if perhaps the bird was trying to lead him *away* from something. Probably, he decided, a nest of young ravens. He had a vague memory that they hatched around this time of year. The bird he was following could be their mother.

He would like to see that nest.

"Caw!" The raven reappeared in a different spot.

Dropping all but one arrow, Casey nocked that one on his bowstring, knowing that the raven would fly off when he did. She did, just as he predicted.

Casey thought hard. The bird had gone first in this direction, then that, then that. Now she had headed another way. In his mind Casey connected all the lines of flight, like a diagram. *Where,* he asked himself, *is the center of all those lines?*

Slipping the leftover arrows into his back pocket—like a quiver—Casey remembered a clearing about a quarter of a mile deeper into the woods. He decided that would be a likely place to find the raven's nest. If he was right, and he went toward it—and if the raven was defending a nest—he'd find her there.

He could get her then.

44

"Why are you just lying here?" Merla screeched into Nashoba's face. "The human is coming! He's a lot closer than before."

"I can't move anymore."

"You have to," cried the raven, pecking the wolf's nose. "You must!"

Nashoba struggled to gather whatever strength he had left. Pushing himself up on his paws, he took one hop-step forward, only to tumble over. From a distance came a burst of light, and then growling thunder.

"*Caw!*" screamed Merla, and leaped into the air.

45

Casey saw the raven rise. This time he was ready. He took his position and aimed—took all the proper steps—and released the arrow.

The bowstring hummed. The white arrow flew.

The bird dropped.

Casey's reaction was astonishment. Had he truly, actually hit the bird? His heart lurched with alarm. For just a second he expected an automated voice to proclaim, *Great shot!* But there were only two sounds Casey heard: the gentle *tip-tap*ping of rain, and his own pounding heart.

Casey searched the trees, waiting for the bird to reappear.

It did not.

Dismay swept through him. Had he *really* killed the raven? He never expected to. It wasn't possible. The idea of it frightened him. *It was just a freak shot,* he told himself. He had not really aimed, had not really intended to kill her.

He *must* have missed.

Must have, he hoped.

Casey moved forward slowly, searching the ground. Maybe the bird was just fooling. She might be faking it. Or was just wounded. He kept looking but saw nothing of the bird. He kept going. Then he stopped. He saw her.

The raven lay on the ground on her back, big black wings extended as if in upside-down flight. Her legs were sticking up, talons in a tight curl.

"Oh my God," Casey whispered. "She's dead."

Horrified, he felt his eyes well with tears. He wiped them away, then looked for his arrow but did not see it. He remembered what his book had said, that an arrow could pierce a jug of sand. This was just a bird. It must have gone right through her.

He felt sick.

He looked around, fearful that someone might have seen what he had done. It was then that he saw what appeared to be large dog footprints. There were also bloodstains. Casey's fright increased. Was the blood from the bird or something else?

He *had* shot two arrows.

Had he killed *two* creatures?

He raised his eyes. In the trees above him, seven ravens were staring down at him.

Alarmed, fearful what the birds might do, Casey nocked another arrow to his string.

With a *whoosh!* the ravens flew off.

Casey went forward, bow and arrow in hand. He looked now this way, then that, ready to shoot until he saw what appeared to be an extremely large dog. It was just lying there.

46

Nashoba heard Merla's last call but did not understand what it meant. He knew only that she had not yet come back. Where was she? Had she left him? Given up on him?

Whimpering quietly, the wolf lifted his head and sniffed. The scent of a human was strong. Extremely close.

Alarmed, he looked around. A human was standing in the rain, staring right at him.

Trying to summon whatever strength he had, Nashoba waited for the human to draw near.

47

Casey saw the dog move its head, so he knew it was alive. He could also see that tracks led from the animal back to where he had seen blood. The dog must be wounded.

Did I hit the dog with my first arrow?

No, that would have been impossible. The dog was too far from his house, too deep among the trees. His arrow could never reach here. But he had hit the raven, hadn't he? And he hadn't expected that. Maybe this dog had been closer to the house, been struck, and dragged itself here.

Did he shoot both creatures?

Moving cautiously, Casey drew closer. He had been taught that wounded animals could and would defend themselves furiously. And the ground was slippery.

He put his bow and three arrows on the ground

but held on to one arrow—daggerlike—thinking he might need it to defend himself. Moving a little closer, he looked into the animal's face.

"What happened to you, fella?" he asked, speaking in a low, soft voice. "You hurt?"

Nashoba raised his large head and gazed at Casey.

He's alive, all right, thought Casey. *Maybe I can help him.*

As Casey looked back, the dog's golden eyes seemed fierce—but maybe it was just pain he saw.

"You're badly hurt, aren't you, boy," Casey said. "What happened? Did . . . I shoot you? Like that raven?"

Nashoba held his gaze.

"If I did," said Casey, "I'm sorry. . . . I didn't mean to do it. Want me to help you?"

Keeping his eyes fixed on the human, Nashoba lowered his head to the ground. His muscles tensed.

Casey saw the bloody paw. He stared. It didn't seem like an arrow wound. But was that why the dog was here?

"I didn't do that, did I, big guy? Did you step

in a trap? Someone else get you?" he asked. "You hurting?"

Nashoba, unblinking, measured the human's nearness.

Casey wiped rainwater from his face. "Do you want some food?" he said. "Some water to drink?"

The thought occurred to him that the dog might have a collar with tags that would identify an owner.

He moved a few steps closer.

Nashoba bared his teeth and growled. Casey halted, stepped back. "That's okay, fella. I understand."

For a few moments Casey stared at the dog, trying to decide what to do.

"Okay," he said. "I know I shouldn't have killed that raven. But I can help you, buddy. Stay here," he said, as if giving a command. "Stay! I'll get you some food and water. Stay!"

Snatching up his bow and arrows, he ran back toward his house.

48

Nashoba was confused. What had just happened? What was the human doing? Why had he run off? Would he come back? Would the human kill him then? Had he killed Merla?

The wolf thought of trying to move, but it was nothing more than a thought. He resigned himself to waiting to learn what the human did next. Besides, he wanted to save every bit of his remaining strength. *I can defend myself,* thought Nashoba. *I can.*

49

It was raining gently but steadily as Casey rushed into his house, through the hall, and into the kitchen. He left the bow and arrows on the kitchen table, then pulled open the fridge door, saw a package of sausages, and yanked it out. He also grabbed a plastic bottle of water and a shallow bowl from a cupboard. From the kitchen he went to the bathroom and opened the cabinet over the sink, scanned the cabinet, and pulled out a tube of ointment, something his mother put on his small cuts and bruises. Hands full, pockets stuffed, telling himself he'd need to clean up his muddy footsteps when he got back, he ran outside. Next second he rushed back to the kitchen. A note pad and pencil were stuck to the fridge door with a magnet. He scribbled:

Walking in forest. Back soon. C

Outside again he raced for the trees. Rain was falling more heavily. The snow was melting.

Just as Casey reached the trees, he was struck with a completely new thought: *What if that dog is the wolf Mr. Souza saw?*

Excited, he ran forward.

50

"Nashoba!"

Startled to hear his name, the wolf looked around, hoping to see Merla. It was Tonagan. In her mouth was a hunk of raw meat. She dropped it right in front of Nashoba's mouth. He said nothing, just grabbed it and bolted it down.

"Where did you get it?" he asked when he was done.

"We caught some of the elk."

Not wishing to ask more, Nashoba said, "What are you doing here?"

"I said I'd come back, didn't I?"

"You mustn't stay," said Nashoba. "You need to get away fast!"

"Why?"

"There's a human coming. He just found me. I think he's coming back so he can kill me. He may have already killed my friend."

"What friend?"

"A raven."

"There's a dead one back among the trees."

"A raven? Dead?"

Tonagan nodded.

Nashoba said, "It must have been that human....
Can't you smell him?"

"Yes . . . but . . ."

"Tonagan, he'll kill you, too. You have to get
away fast! The pups need you."

The two wolves gazed at each other. "Go!"
Nashoba cried. "Fast as you can!"

Tonagan turned, halted, looked back, whispered
"Good-bye," and ran off.

Nashoba watched her bounding away among
the trees. He stared for a long time, until he could
no longer see her.

As Nashoba lay there, he began to feel new
energy from the food he'd just eaten. *That human
killed Merla,* he thought. Then he told himself, *I
have one more kill in me.*

Hoping it was true, he closed his eyes and
waited.

51

Holding tightly to the sausage, water, and bowl, Casey burst into the clearing. The dog—or was it a wolf?—was lying perfectly still, eyes closed.

The boy halted. *He's dead,* he thought, *I'm too late,* only to see the animal's sides heave. "Good boy!" he said. "You're breathing."

He went forward a few steps.

Hearing the voice, Nashoba opened his eyes and lifted his snout. His staring eyes, dark and deep, brought Casey to a sudden stop. His dad's words, *I wouldn't mess with a wolf,* popped into his head.

If he's a wolf, the boy told himself, *a wounded wolf, he might be dangerous.* He studied Nashoba. "You a wolf?" he called, asking himself as much as Nashoba.

Nashoba's eyes, giving no hint as to his thoughts, held steady.

What's he doing? Casey wondered. *Is he going to attack me?*

Nashoba, keeping his eyes on the boy, told himself, *Wait until he's closer. Wait.*

Casey, uncertain what to do, remained in place, heart hammering. "You look in a bad way, fella," he said.

Nashoba made no response.

Casey went forward two tentative steps. "You're going to be okay," he said, trying to sound reassuring. "I've got food." He held it up.

Nashoba, eyes unblinking, remained motionless.

"Is it okay that I help you?" asked Casey, wishing the animal would give some hint as to what he might do. *He doesn't seem dangerous,* Casey told himself.

There was no movement from Nashoba.

"Just want to be your friend," Casey offered.

He took another step forward, even as he prepared to jump back if the wolf did anything threatening.

Nashoba remained still, eyes steady.

Closer now, Casey stretched out his hand—it was trembling slightly—with the sausages.

Nashoba, intent on the boy's face, told himself to be patient. *Wait until he's nearer, until he's nearer . . .*

Crouching, Casey tossed the meat so it landed in front of Nashoba's nose.

Though Nashoba understood he was being offered food, he did not look at it. Instead he kept his eyes fixed on the boy, telling himself, *He killed Merla.*

"Go on, big boy," Casey urged. "Eat it. It's good for you."

The smell of food was too enticing. After a few moments Nashoba reached forward, took the sausage into his mouth, and swallowed it quickly.

"Atta boy!" cried Casey, his tension easing. "Want some water?" He edged nearer. On his knees in the thin snow, he carefully set the bowl down where the sausages had been. He emptied the bottled water into it—even tipped the bowl up slightly. That done, he shuffled back.

Nashoba hesitated, then lapped the water.

"Good, isn't it, boy?" said Casey. Remaining on his knees, he said, "Still hungry, fella? Thirsty? Should I get some more?"

Nashoba stared, trying to make sense of the human. Was he being kind—like Merla—or was he going to kill him?

Casey took the tube of ointment out of his back pocket and held it up. "If you'd let me put some of this stuff on your paw, big guy, it might help." He unscrewed the cap and held it up as if the wolf might make sense of it.

When the wolf made no response, Casey, feeling increasingly sure of himself, shuffled forward on his knees. He stretched toward Nashoba's paw. Nashoba kept his eyes on the human's face.

Casey squeezed the tube until a thick blob of yellow ointment plopped down onto the wound. He sat back. "Okay?" he asked.

The wolf gave no reaction.

Leaning in, Casey put out his fingers and began to smear it about the wound.

That was when Nashoba lurched forward and bit into Casey's hand.

"Hey!" Casey cried, and tried to pull back.

Nashoba clamped down tighter.

"Let me go!" cried the frightened boy, unable to

pull away. Awkwardly, he tried to get his feet under himself to gain leverage. "You're hurting me!" he screamed. "Let me go!"

Nashoba had no understanding of what the human was saying. It sounded like pleading. He didn't care. But as he held on to the human's hand, he suddenly recalled how his pups had mouthed him when they begged for food and life.

It was as if he, Nashoba, had become young, and this human was old. And when he looked into the boy's face, he saw fright, the kind of fright he had recently felt.

I can't kill him, he told himself. And he opened his mouth and let the boy go.

Casey snatched back his hand, cupped it in his other hand, and examined it. His skin was barely broken. He sucked on a spot of blood and looked reproachfully at the animal. "Why'd you do that?" he cried, tears coming from hurt and shock. "I was just trying to help you!"

Nashoba put his head down between his paws but continued to stare at the boy.

Casey's hurt subsided. "My fault," he said. "Guess

that stuff stung a bit. Sorry. Just trying to help."
He smeared his tears while pushing wet hair away
from his face. All the while, he continued to study
Nashoba. "You know what?" he said. "You have
really sad eyes."

Clumsily, the boy got to his feet. "Want me to
get more food?"

Nashoba made no response.

"Be right back," said Casey, and he started to run.

52

Nashoba lay quietly. *I am old,* he thought. *I can't kill.*

53

Home again, Casey rummaged in the fridge. This
time he found bacon, a couple of hamburger patties,

three pizza slices wrapped in aluminum foil, and another bottle of water.

He raced back to Nashoba. Once there, he dumped all the food in front of the animal, then stood in front of him while Nashoba devoured everything. He offered more water, too, which Nashoba drank.

"You want more?" Casey asked. Not getting any more answers than before, he said. "I'll get some." He turned toward home. As he stepped from among the trees, he saw his father's truck in the driveway.

54

Nashoba tried to make sense of all that had happened: Why had the human fed him? He had never heard of such a thing. Was it because he was young? Would the human come back? Would he bring more food? Or would he, this time, kill him? Was this human really the one who killed Merla? No, he couldn't be. He was kind.

Then who killed the raven?

He didn't know.

He wished he understood humans.

What Nashoba did know was that with all the food he had eaten, his strength was returning. Even his paw hurt less.

Working to stand up, he was much more successful. No longer shaky, or dizzy, he took a few tentative steps. Though there was still pain, he could tolerate it better. He could walk.

Nashoba wished he had not told Tonagan to run off. She would tell the pack what he had said about the human, and they would move away fast. He would never be able to catch up with her or his wolves again.

He stood quietly, gathering strength. The rain was starting to taper off. Mist drifted through the trees. *I can move,* Nashoba told himself. Even so, he didn't. He was trying to decide if he should wait for the human to come back. Maybe he, like Merla, could be a friend.

55

When Casey walked into the house, his dad greeted him. "Hey there. Have a good walk?"

"Guess what, Dad?"

"What's that?"

"I found that wolf."

"What are you talking about?"

"The one Mr. Souza talked about. It's true!" As fast as he could, he told his dad what had happened.

When he was done, Casey said, "You don't believe me, do you? Look." He held out his hand. The teeth marks were still visible.

"Looks to me like you lost two arrows, maybe shot a raven—which was dumb as well as lucky—and you came too close to a hurt animal. And he bit you. You're lucky he didn't break your hand."

"It's a wolf, Dad. I'm sure it is."

"Can you show me?"

"Sure."

"Let's go."

They left the house. The rain had stopped. In its place, gray mist moved through the air. Casey turned toward the woods, but his dad was heading for the garage.

"Where you going?" Casey called.

"A hurt dog—which you say is a wolf—I'm getting my gun."

"Dad, you don't need it! He won't hurt you. He's nice."

"I'm sorry. The kindest thing you can do is to put a wounded dog out of its misery."

"Dad . . . !"

"Let me be the judge. Case, you haven't been very wise, have you? Okay, you're a teenager, but come on, you've acted like a little kid." He saw his father enter the garage.

"Dad," he called, "I may have killed a raven, but I saved that wolf!"

As he waited for his father, he looked around and saw the arrow he had first shot. It was there, exposed by melting snow. A wave of relief washed through Casey. He had not shot the wolf.

His dad returned with his .223 rifle.

"Dad, look! I found that arrow. It never reached the woods. It wasn't me who got the wolf."

"Fine," said his father. "Show me the dog."

Reluctantly, Casey led the way into the woods. His father, rifle in hand, walked by his side. They trudged silently through trees. The air was cloudy, shrouding everything, taking away all forms. It was as if the world had begun to change shape, to melt. When Casey glanced back, he could no longer see where he had come from. He paused, checked to find his bearings, walked on, and found the clearing

Nashoba was not there.

"He was right here," Casey insisted.

"You sure this is the spot?" his dad asked.

"He was. Look, paw prints. And over here: blood."

"Okay. Then where is he?"

Casey, relieved, said, "I have no idea."

"Where's the raven?"

"Over there."

They walked some fifteen more yards, when Casey spied an arrow. He ran and picked it up. There was blood on it. But there was no raven.

He looked up at his dad. "Maybe I only wounded it," he said, holding up the arrow.

"You sure you weren't just playing your game?"

"They were *real,* Dad!" cried Casey.

"Well, whatever," said his dad. "Let's go home."

Casey followed his father, trying to make sense of what had happened.

56

"Want to set up a target?" his father asked as they approached the house. "Start practicing with the bow?"

"Just need to check something," said Casey.

He hurried to his room and turned on his computer. Bowhunter came on, filling the screen with its jungle scene: green vines, immense flowers, tall grasses, and dangling snakes. He waited for half an hour. No wolf appeared. No raven.

Where, Casey wondered, *did the raven and wolf go?*

He heard his dad call, "Case? We going to practice?"

Casey turned off the computer and went out. It was the last time he looked at that game.

57

Nashoba walked slowly among the damp trees, up and out of the valley. Though limping, he moved steadily into higher country, away from the human. His thick fur kept him from feeling the rain or the mist.

When he was far above, he paused and looked back. A white cloud lay cupped in the valley below, hiding it from view. Where Nashoba stood, there was still snow, but it was melting. In the bare spots, yellow snow lilies had sprung up, as if the rays of the sun had come not from above but from below.

As Nashoba remained in place, a swarm of smells swept up from the valley. There was the scent of rain and the scent of growing grasses, budding bushes, new mushrooms, and decaying wood. He sniffed the scent of a foul porcupine plodding about somewhere. He noted the fragrance of pinecones being nibbled by a black squirrel in a high lodgepole pine.

He heard mice moving underground. He heard a black bear lumbering among the trees announcing he had awoken from a long winter's rest. He heard the sound of running water. A rising breeze caused the sap-thin trees to creak and crack, as if chilly limbs were stretching.

When he looked up into the clear mountain sky, he saw flitting chickadees, a pair of gray pigeons, and a fat and furry bumblebee. Canada geese were flying in a V formation toward the north, a welcome sign that spring was coming.

Highest of all, a flight of eight ravens—their great black wings beating slowly—flew by. Nashoba stared. Was Merla there? He lifted his head and howled, once, twice, three times. No answer came.

The birds vanished.

Remembering what the raven had said—*Wise creatures live by questions*—Nashoba asked first, *Where shall I go?*

He could almost hear Merla saying, *You have already come to where you shall go.*

But what shall I be?

What you already are, an old wolf.

A question? An answer?

Nashoba went on, limping, but alive.